The Petsitters Club

1. Jilly the Kid

More animal adventure with The Petsitters Club!

2. The Cat Burglar

Look out for:

3. Donkey Rescue
4. Snake Alarm

Calling all animal lovers!
Look out for Young Hippo Animal:

Hands Off Our Hens!
Jennifer Curry

Big Puss, Little Mouse
Kara May

TESSA KRAILING

The Petsitters Club

1. Jilly the Kid

Illustrated by Jan Lewis

Scholastic Children's Books,
Commonwealth House, 1-19 New Oxford Street,
London WC1A 1NU, UK
a division of Scholastic Ltd
London ~ New York ~ Toronto ~ Sydney ~ Auckland

Published in the UK by Scholastic Ltd, 1997

Text copyright © Tessa Krailing, 1997
Illustrations copyright © Jan Lewis, 1997

ISBN 0 590 13918 5

Printed by Cox & Wyman Ltd, Reading, Berks

10 9 8 7 6 5 4 3 2 1

Chapter 1

A Brilliant Idea

"I hate gardening!" Sam sat back on her heels. "Especially weeding. Ugh!"

Just then Matthew White came down the road, being pulled along by a small mongrel dog. Matthew was in Sam's class at school. When the dog stopped to sniff at the gatepost, Matthew looked over the hedge and said, "Hello, Sam. Why are you weeding this garden? You don't live here."

"No, Mrs Bratby does." Sam wiped a hand across her hot face. "She heard about our community service scheme and asked Mr Grantham to send somebody round."

Mr Grantham was their headmaster. He was very keen on all the kids in his school doing something for the community where they lived. They got points for each job, provided the person they'd worked for signed a special form. Then at the end of term the points were added up and whoever had done the most jobs received a special cup.

Sam wanted to win that cup. She thought it would look great on the mantelshelf. That's why, when Mr Grantham had asked for someone to weed Mrs Bratby's garden, she had put up her hand.

Now she was beginning to wish she hadn't. "Mrs Bratby's so *fussy*," she told Matthew. "She gets mad if I miss a single weed. I hate this job."

"I'm walking this dog for the old lady who lives next door," Matthew said. "His name's Bruno."

At the sound of his name Bruno lost interest in the gatepost and bounded up to the hedge, wagging his tail.

"I love animals." Sam leaned over to pat Bruno's head. "You are lucky, Matthew. I'd much rather walk somebody's dog than do their gardening."

"Why don't you, then? My dad says there are a lot of dogs around that never get taken out for walks."

"Poor things," said Sam, stroking Bruno's silky ears.

"He says some dogs are left alone in the house all day while their owners are out at work. It's no wonder they get bored and start barking. Then the neighbours complain."

"That's awful," said Sam, horrified. "Can't he do something about it? After all, he's a policeman."

Matthew shook his head. "He says the owners don't mean to be cruel. They just don't think."

"Then they *should* think! They could easily ask someone to go in during the day and feed the dog ... and let it out in the garden ... and *talk* to it." She straightened up. "Matthew, I've just had a brilliant idea!"

"Oh, yes?" he said cautiously.

"Why don't we start up a sort of club for looking after people's pets? Not just dogs, but cats and gerbils and hamsters – any kind of pet that's left alone a lot. That would be a really useful service, much better than gardening. We could call it a – a Petsitters Club, and we could still get points for it!"

Matthew thought hard for a moment.

He was a slow thinker and whenever he thought his face became all scrunched up with concentration.

At last he nodded. "Okay."

Sam glanced over her shoulder, afraid that Mrs Bratby might come out of her house and catch her talking to Matthew. Wasting time, she'd call it. "Come round to my house after tea," she said. "We'll talk about it then."

But when Matthew turned to go he found that he had a lead attached to a collar but no dog. "Where's Bruno?" he asked.

"I don't know. Perhaps he –" Sam's eyes grew wide with horror. "Matthew, look! He's come into the garden. He must have wriggled through the hedge. Oh, no! He's lifting his leg against the apple tree. Mrs Bratby will be *furious*!"

She ran towards Bruno, waving her arms.
"Bruno, stop that. Bad dog."

Bruno thought it was a fine old game.
He raced round and round the garden,
wagging his tail and barking as if to say,
"Come on, chase me."

"Oh, shush!" pleaded Sam. "Mrs
Bratby will hear you."

Too late. Mrs Bratby had already heard. She burst out of her front door, shouting, "Get off my rose-bed, you horrible hound. Go away, go away! I hate dogs! Whoever let that dog inside my garden will be sorry. Just wait till I catch you..."

By now Sam wasn't sure who Mrs Bratby was chasing – Bruno or herself. So she started running *with* Bruno instead of after him, and they both reached the front gate at the same time.

Matthew opened the gate to let them out.

"Good riddance!" yelled Mrs Bratby. "And don't ever come back."

"But Mrs Bratby –" Sam pulled out the community service form from her jeans pocket. "You haven't signed this..."

"No, and I don't intend to! In fact, I shall tell your headmaster exactly what I think of his stupid scheme. Pah!"

Mrs Bratby went back inside her bungalow and slammed the door.

"Bad luck, Sam." Matthew bent down to slip the collar over Bruno's head. "That's the trouble with animals. You never know what they're going to do next. Are you sure you want to go ahead with this petsitting idea?"

"Quite sure," Sam said firmly. She started off down the road. "See you later, Matthew."

Chapter 2

Ready for Business

While Sam was washing up the tea things she told her dad, "Matthew White's coming round soon. We're having a meeting. You don't mind, do you?"

"Mmm," said Dad.

"Does that mean mmm, yes? Or mmm, no?"

"No. I mean yes. Er, I don't know."

Sam turned round to look at him. He was sitting at the kitchen table, working. That is, he was drawing little men with funny faces and putting speech bubbles over their heads. Some people, she knew, wouldn't call that work. But it was how her dad earned his living, drawing comic strips for magazines.

He tore the sheet of paper off his pad, screwed it up and flung it on the floor.

"No good?" Sam asked sympathetically.

Dad sighed. "I seem to have run out of ideas. Sorry, what was it you just asked me?"

"If you minded Matthew coming here for a meeting?"

"Oh. No, I don't mind..." He started drawing again.

"We'll talk in the den. Then we won't disturb you."

"Mmm."

When Matthew arrived he wasn't alone. He had brought his best mate Jovan Roy. "Jo wants to join our club," Matthew told Sam.

Sam glanced doubtfully at Jovan. He didn't look very enthusiastic. In fact he was hanging back on the doorstep as if joining a Petsitters Club was the last thing he wanted to do.

"Jo's dad is a vet," Matthew reminded her.

Sam brightened at once. "That means if a pet gets sick while we're looking after it Jo can give us expert advice. Come on in."

But then she saw that Jovan wasn't the only person Matthew had brought along. His young sister Katie stood behind him on the step, clutching a jamjar.

"What's she doing here?" Sam demanded.

Matthew groaned. "She followed us. I couldn't stop her."

"I heard Matthew and Jo talking," Katie said. "And I want to join as well."

"I'm afraid you're too young," Sam explained as kindly as she could. "It's a very responsible job, looking after people's pets."

"But I'm an expert too. I'm an expert on creepy-crawlies." Katie held up the jar to show Sam what was inside. "This is Monty. He's a centipede."

"Ugh!" Sam backed away.

"You see?" Katie said triumphantly. "Supposing someone asks you to look after their lonely stick insect. It'd be no use saying 'Ugh!' then. You need ME to look after the creepy-crawlies."

"Oh, all right," Sam agreed, although she thought it very unlikely they would ever be asked to look after a lonely stick insect. "You'd better come in, all of you."

She led them into the den, which was the smallest, untidiest, cosiest room in the house. "This is where my dad usually works, but this evening he's working in the kitchen, so we can have our meeting in here."

Katie took the lid off her jamjar. "I'd better let Monty out for a walk. He needs plenty of exercise with all those legs."

"Well, okay," Sam said reluctantly. "But don't let him go under the furniture or you may never find him again."

The others joined Sam at her father's drawing-board. "First thing we have to do," she said, turning over a clean sheet of paper, "is to put an advertisement in the newsagent's window so that people know about our service."

Matthew looked doubtfully at the sheet of paper. "It's a bit big," he said. "Usually people put their ads on postcards."

"It's got to be big to grab people's attention." Sam picked up a felt-tip pen and started writing in large letters:

TOO BUSY TO FEED YOUR CAT?
TOO OLD TO WALK YOUR DOG?

"That sounds rude," said Matthew. "People don't like being called old, even if they are."

Sam drew a line through the word "old" and put "tired" instead. "Now, we'll have to give a telephone number…"

Nobody seemed keen for their telephone number to be given.

"Oh, all right. I'll put mine," said Sam. "I hope people don't ring up while I'm at school, that's all. Still, Dad never answers the phone while he's working, so it should be okay."

"Don't forget about the creepy-crawlies," Katie reminded her, rescuing Monty before he could crawl under the armchair.

"And don't forget about Jo's dad being a vet," said Matthew.

Jovan said unhappily, "My dad's very busy. I don't think he'll want to be bothered—"

"Oh, we shan't need to *bother* him," Sam interrupted. "You must have learned a lot about being a vet, Jo, just from watching your dad work. I know I've learned a lot about drawing cartoons from watching *my* dad work. Wait, I'll do a funny dog picture on the advertisement. That'll make people take notice."

When she had finished, the advertisement looked like this:

"There!" Sam put down her pen. "I reckon the phone will start ringing as soon as this ad goes in the newsagent's window. Let's take it round there now."

Chapter 3

We're Not Babysitters!

Jovan wasn't happy. He wasn't happy at all. He liked Sam and he liked Matthew and he liked the idea of belonging to a club.

But not to a Petsitters Club.

The trouble was that he didn't like animals.

In fact he was scared of them.

People seemed to think, because his father was a vet, that he must know a lot about animals. Well, he did. He knew that cats could scratch, dogs could bite – and even hamsters could give you a nasty nip with their sharp front teeth if they wanted to. Up till now, as far as possible, he had tried to keep away from animals.

But now he found himself belonging to a club whose whole purpose was to look after the wretched creatures!

Jovan groaned.

"Something wrong?" asked his mother.

It was late afternoon on Friday and they were sitting in the front room, watching TV. It was one of those wildlife programmes that Mum liked so much, full of lions eating their prey and monkeys scratching themselves. Just watching them made him feel itchy.

"I've got a bit of a headache," said Jovan. "I think I'll go upstairs to my room."

"That's right, have a nice rest." Mum turned her gaze back to the TV screen, where a python was squeezing its dinner to death.

But while he was crossing the hall the doorbell rang. He answered it to find Matthew on the doorstep, panting hard as if he had been running.

"Sam called me," Matthew said. "She wants us to go over to her place. She says it's urgent."

Jovan stared at him. "Is it about our ad?"

"Don't know. She didn't say. Come on."

Matthew was already halfway down the path. Jovan knew he had to follow him: it would look strange if he didn't.

With a sinking heart he told his mother where he was going and promised he wouldn't be long.

Sam came to the front door. "Something's gone wrong," she said. "Come into the den and I'll tell you about it."

What could have happened? Jovan wondered as she led them through her big, gloomy house. Too many pets? Too few? Or perhaps none at all? He began to feel more hopeful.

Sam closed the door of the den. "There was a phone call today while I was out and my dad answered it."

"But you said he wouldn't," said Matthew. "You said he never answered it when he was working."

"He's hit a bad patch. The ideas won't come. So he answered it and took a message. Look."

She showed them the message scrawled on a piece of paper torn from her father's note pad.

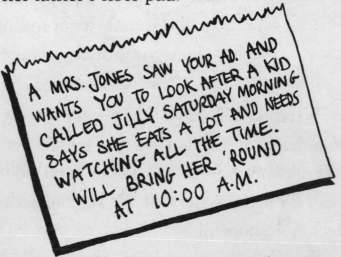

A MRS. JONES SAW YOUR AD. AND WANTS YOU TO LOOK AFTER A KID CALLED JILLY SATURDAY MORNING SAYS SHE EATS A LOT AND NEEDS WATCHING ALL THE TIME. WILL BRING HER 'ROUND AT 10:00 A.M.

"It's a girl!" Matthew said, disgusted. "Mrs Jones couldn't have read the notice properly. She thinks we're *baby*sitters!"

"That's what my dad thinks too," said Sam. "He was a bit annoyed I hadn't told him about putting the ad in the window, but now he thinks we're offering to babysit he doesn't mind."

"Well, *I* mind!" said Matthew. "I'm not spending my Saturday morning looking after a little kid. The message says she needs watching all the time. That means she's naughty. I've got trouble enough with Katie."

"I heard that!" Katie's face appeared at the open window. "And *I* don't want to look after a little kid either, especially one who eats a lot. I bet she's fat as a pig. Yuck!"

She climbed in
and sat on the
window-sill.

"Saturday's tomorrow," said Matthew. "And we've already got a dog to walk and a rabbit to feed. We'll just have to call this Mrs Jones back—"

"We can't," said Sam. "Dad didn't get the number."

Matthew groaned. "There must be hundreds of Joneses in the telephone book. That means we're stuck with her wretched kid."

"I'll do it," said Jovan.

Sam and Katie stared at him.

"I'll look after her," he said, thinking he'd much rather look after a little girl than take a dog for a walk. At least little girls didn't have sharp, pointed teeth – unless, of course, they were vampires!

He added, "It's a service, after all. We'll still get points for it."

Sam cheered up at once. "Oh, well … as long as you don't mind, Jo."

"I'll come at nine-thirty," he said, "so that I'm here when she arrives."

"What about me?" demanded Katie.

"Nobody's asked us to look after any creepy-crawlies," said Sam. Then she saw Katie's look of disappointment. "If you like you can come here and catch as many spiders as you can. We've got masses and I hate them. So that'll be a service too. I'll get my dad to sign your form."

"Oh, great!" said Katie.

Which is why, when the doorbell rang on the following morning, Jovan answered it alone. Sam and Matthew were out dog-walking; Katie was upstairs in the bathroom hunting for spiders; and Sam's dad was tearing his hair out in the kitchen, still trying to think up a new idea for a cartoon.

Mrs Jones was a thin woman with a worried expression. "Are you the pet-sitting service? You seem rather young. Still, I suppose you'll have to do. I warn you, though, she's a little terror."

Jovan couldn't speak. He was too busy staring at the small, black-and-white, four-legged creature attached to a length of rope held by Mrs Jones.

"I only got her Thursday," she went on. "I have this large garden, you see, and I thought she would save me having to mow the grass. But it hasn't worked out as I'd imagined. She's caused so much damage, it's been a nightmare." She thrust the rope into Jovan's hands. "Here, take her. I don't know when I'll be back. Probably never. You can keep her for all I care..."

She turned and ran down the path.

Jovan stared after her. He couldn't believe this was happening to him. They must have misunderstood the message. Jilly was a kid all right, but she wasn't a little girl.

She was a GOAT!

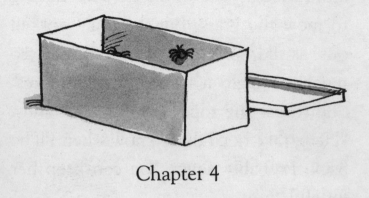

Chapter 4

The Little Terror

Katie was having a wonderful time. So far she had caught five spiders, four of them in the bathroom. Now they were all scuttling around in the cardboard box she had found in Sam's bedroom. It had contained a jigsaw, but she emptied the pieces on to the bed and made some small holes in the lid so that the spiders could breathe. Soon she would take them into the garden and let them go free.

She heard the doorbell and guessed it must be Mrs Jones. "I shan't go downstairs," she said to herself, "in case Jovan makes me play with that little kid."

Ah, there was another spider! A huge one this time, with furry legs.

The box was getting overcrowded. She would have to take it down to the garden. If she was careful she might be able to creep downstairs without anyone hearing...

She was halfway across the landing when from the hall below came the most terrific CRASH!

"Jo?" Katie peered over the bannisters. "Jo, is that you?"

"Help!" Jovan's voice sounded as if he was in pain.

Katie ran down the stairs to the hall. To her amazement she saw Jovan lying on the floor, surrounded by bits of blue china. "Did you break something?" she asked.

"A vase," Jovan gasped. "On the table. But it wasn't me that broke it. It was Jilly."

"The little kid?" She helped Jovan to his feet. "How did it happen?"

"She got away from me." Jovan struggled to his feet. "She's very strong, you'd be surprised. As soon as she started pulling at the rope—"

"Rope?" Katie stared at him. "You mean you had her on a piece of rope, like a lead? Poor little kid. Where is she now?"

"She ran off somewhere. Into the den, I think."

At that moment there came another crash, this time from inside the den, followed by the sound of paper tearing. Katie marched purposefully towards the open door and stuck her head round. "Now look here, Jilly," she began – and then stopped.

Sam's dad's drawing-board lay sideways on the floor, while the large sheet of paper attached to it was being torn off and eaten by a small, black-and-white goat.

"Oh!" A pleased smile spread over Katie's face. "*That* kind of a kid."

Jovan peered over her shoulder into the room. "*Now* look what she's done! She's a little terror. Mrs Jones did warn me."

"I think she's sweet." Katie, still holding her box of spiders, went over to Jilly. She stroked the kid's nose and Jilly butted her gently. "Oh, she has a lovely little face."

Jovan was too busy clearing up the mess to look. He righted the fallen drawing-board and stared at the torn paper with dismay. "Sam's dad will be furious. First the vase ... and now this. It's a wonder he hasn't come to find out what all the noise was about."

"Sam said he was working on a new cartoon. I expect he's too busy to notice." Katie watched uneasily as Jilly started nibbling at the box containing the spiders. "I think she's hungry. Let's take her into the garden."

"Okay," said Jovan. "How do we get there?"

"Through the back door, I expect."

"We can't go into the kitchen," he said. "Sam's father's in there."

"Well, if he's too busy to notice the noise Jilly's been making I don't suppose he'll notice us going through the kitchen. Come on."

But when Katie took hold of the rope, Jilly dug all four hooves into the carpet and refused to budge.

Katie sighed. "You'd better give her a push, Jo."

Jovan approached Jilly's rear with caution. He put both hands on her rump and pushed hard. Startled, Jilly took off with a leap and they all three shot through the hall at top speed and into the kitchen, where Sam's dad sat hunched over his notepad.

"Excuse us," Jovan said as they sped past him. "We're just going into the garden."

"Mmm?"

"The garden," Jovan repeated.

But by this time they were safely outside.

Jilly, finding herself in the middle of a vegetable patch, came to a sudden stop. She lowered her head and started nibbling some sprout tops.

Katie looked around her. "Wow, this is a really wild garden! I reckon we could let Jilly go free. She can't do any harm here. There's nothing to damage except a few mouldy old vegetables."

"As long as she can't get out," Jovan agreed cautiously.

"There's a hedge all round. She can't possibly get out." Katie dropped the rope, leaving Jilly happily browsing among the sprouts. "Now I can set my spiders free."

"Better take them as far away from Jilly as possible," Jovan warned, "or she might gobble them up."

Katie carried the cardboard box down to the end of the garden and took off the lid. "There you are, my darlings," she murmured. "You'll be much happier here than in that slippery old bathroom."

She watched her captives scuttle off into the undergrowth, certain they wore happy smiles on their little black spider faces.

When she returned to the vegetable patch she found Jovan sitting on the back doorstep with his eyes closed, enjoying the sunshine.

"You know, this isn't so bad," he said, sounding quite cheerful. "I don't think I shall mind this petsitting business after all. It's really quite easy once you get the hang of it."

"Of course it is." Katie was surprised he should have any doubts. She sat down beside him. "Where's Jilly now?"

"Over by the hedge. I think she got sick of eating vegetables."

"I don't blame her. I get sick of eating vegetables too." Katie looked round the garden. "I can't see her. Are you sure she's there?"

"Well, she was a minute ago." Jovan opened his eyes. "Oh, no! She must have eaten her way through the hedge ... and now she's gone!"

Chapter 5

A Trail of Disaster

When Sam and Matthew had finished walking the dogs – one was Bruno, the other a Yorkshire terrier called Fred – they returned them to their grateful owners and went straight back to Sam's house.

"I wonder how Jo's been getting on with Jilly," Sam said as they walked up the front path.

"Funny that," said Matthew. "I'd never have thought old Jo would want to look after a little kid. I was amazed when he volunteered."

"Me too," Sam agreed.

Inside the hall she stood still, listening. "I can't hear anything. I wonder where they are."

Matthew pointed to the broken china. "Looks like somebody broke something."

"Oh, that's only the present Aunt Cynthia gave us last Christmas," Sam said. "Dad hated it. He'll be glad it's broken."

"Jo?" called Matthew. "Katie? Where are you?"

Nobody answered.

"That's funny." Sam opened the kitchen door and looked in. Her father was still sitting at the table, his head

buried in his hands. "Have you seen Jo and Katie?" she asked him.

"Mmm?"

"Jo and Katie. We left them here about an hour ago."

"I think I did catch sight of them," Dad said vaguely. "They went into the garden."

"Did they have a little kid with them?"

"They may have done." He frowned. "Yes, now you come to mention it, I believe I did see a little kid."

"Thanks, Dad." She turned to Matthew. "I expect they're playing hide-and-seek. Ours is a great garden for hide-and-seek. Let's go and find them."

But the garden appeared to be empty, and although Matthew called, "Jo? Katie?" several times, and Sam looked in all the best hiding places, they eventually had to give up.

"It's very strange," said Sam, as they turned back to the house. "I wonder where they can have got to?"

"Perhaps they took Jilly for a walk." Matthew stopped dead. "Did you hear that?"

"Hear what?"

"Hoofbeats outside ... and someone yelling..."

Next moment a small, black-and-white goat came crashing through the hedge, dragging Katie on the end of a rope and followed by a hot-looking Jovan. Sam and Matthew watched in amazement as the three of them raced twice round the garden, between the bushes, through the long grass and over the vegetable patch. Finally they came to a halt when the goat decided to eat some turnip tops.

"What on earth – ?" began Sam.

"This is Jilly," said Katie, breathing hard.

Sam said, "But I thought Jilly was a little –" Suddenly the penny dropped. "Oh, *that* kind of a kid!"

"She's a terror," panted Jovan. "We've had the most awful time."

"You wouldn't believe what she did—"

"Everywhere we went she left a trail of disaster..."

"Calm down," ordered Sam. "Get your breath back and then tell me what happened."

Jovan wiped a hand across his sweating brow. "Well, first of all she got out of this garden and down the street..."

"And into the greengrocer's," said Katie. "She stole two apples and a bunch of bananas. The greengrocer was *furious...*"

"And then she went down Green Avenue," said Jovan. "You know, where all those posh bungalows are..."

"With the beautiful gardens..."

"And into the big one on the corner..."

Sam groaned. "Not Mrs Bratby's, where I used to do the gardening?"

"That's right," said Jovan. "She came out and chased us."

"She was even furiouser than the greengrocer," said Katie. "She said first it was dogs messing up her lawn and now goats and how she hated all animals."

"Children as well," said Jovan. "Luckily Jilly stopped to eat some roses."

Sam groaned again. "Not Mrs Bratby's precious roses?"

"And that's when we caught her," said Katie, triumphant.

Sam glanced at Jilly, who was still peacefully munching turnip tops. "How long are we supposed to look after her?"

Jovan looked uncomfortable. "I'm not sure…"

"What do you mean, you're not sure?" Sam demanded.

"I have a feeling Mrs Jones isn't coming back."

Matthew stared at him. "Why not?"

"She seemed a bit fed up with Jilly,"
Jovan explained. "She only got her two
days ago, to keep the grass short in her
garden, but it hasn't worked out the way
she expected. She said we could keep her
for all she cared."

Sam and Matthew exchanged a
worried look.

"That's okay," Katie said cheerfully.

"Jilly can keep the grass short in your garden instead, Sam. It needs cutting. Of course, you'll have to mend the hole in the hedge."

Sam looked doubtful. "I don't know what my dad will say."

"He won't notice," said Katie. "He didn't notice when we brought her through the kitchen."

Sam sighed. "Oh, well, I suppose we'll have to keep her for the time being. But I don't know anything about goats. For a start, what do they eat?"

"Roses," said Katie. "And paper and sprout tops and apples and bananas..."

"I meant what is she *supposed* to eat?" said Sam. "You'd better ask your father, Jo. It looks like we're going to need his help after all."

Chapter 6

An Unexpected Visitor

Jovan found his father in the surgery. "Dad," he said, breathless from hurrying. "What do goats eat?"

"Goats?" Mr Roy stopped clipping the toenails of a large bull-terrier to stare at his son. "Well, they eat hay mostly. Why do you want to know?"

Jovan explained the situation, while at

the same time keeping a careful eye on
the bull-terrier. He hardly ever visited
the surgery if he could possibly help it.
You never knew what fearsome creatures
you might meet there.

When he had heard the story Mr Roy said, "These people who buy a goat instead of a lawnmower make me sick. It just shows how little they know about animals. Goats don't like being left on their own. If your friend Sam wants to keep this goat she should get another female to keep it company."

"I don't think she wants to keep it for ever," said Jovan.

"In that case you'd better tell her to go and see Pete Duffy. He keeps a herd of goats on some land at the end of Station Road. With luck he may have room for one more."

A piece of extra-hard toenail flew into the air. The bull-terrier growled menacingly.

"Give me a hand, son," said Mr Roy. "If you come closer and get a firm grip on his jaw—"

"Sorry, Dad," said Jovan, backing away. "I've got to go now. Sam's waiting for the answer."

By four o'clock that afternoon there was still no sign of Mrs Jones. The four Petsitters sat on the back step of Sam's house, watching Jilly eat grass. Matthew had tethered her with a long rope tied to a tree, and for the moment at least she seemed content.

Sam sighed. "If everyone leaves their pets with us for good we shall end up running a zoo."

Katie said, "Oh, great! Can I be in charge of the insectarium?"

"If you want."

"I'll go and see what I can catch." She jumped up from the step and ran off down the garden.

Matthew looked at the grazing Jilly. "You know, she's really rather a nice little kid when she's behaving herself."

"Oh, she's fine," Sam agreed, "as long as there's someone around to keep an eye on her. But I daren't leave her alone for a second."

"Goats like company," Jovan said. "Least, that's what my dad told me."

"That's all very well," said Sam. "But what's going to happen tonight? I can't take her upstairs to bed with me. And on Monday I have to go to school."

"Oh, she'll be all right now she's tethered," Matthew said.

Sam looked doubtfully at the rope. It was an old washing-line she had found in the shed and rather worn in places. If Jilly gave it a good hard pull...

"Sam, Sam!" Katie came running back up the garden. "You've got a visitor. A lady just rang your front doorbell – and guess what! It's that lady with the roses, the one who chased us."

"Not Mrs Bratby!" Sam turned pale. "What does she want?"

"I expect she's looking for Katie and me," said Jovan. "How did she know where to find us?"

"Can't think," said Sam. "But if nobody answers the door she'll go away."

"Your dad just answered it," said Katie. "I heard him ask her inside."

Sam groaned. "I'd better go and see what's happening."

She raced through the kitchen and into the hall, the others following. When they heard voices coming from the den they halted, staring at each other.

"What's she saying?" whispered Matthew.

"I can't hear," said Sam. "I'd better go in and find out. The rest of you stay out of sight."

She opened the door to see Mrs Bratby, in a rose-patterned dress with a flower-trimmed hat to match, seated on the sofa in front of the window.

Dad swung round, looking relieved.

"Ah, here's my daughter now. I'll leave you to ask her yourself. You'll excuse me if I get back to work?" Without waiting for a reply he left the room.

Ask me what? Sam wondered. She stood in front of Mrs Bratby, not daring to say a word.

Mrs Bratby adjusted her hat and began in a grand voice,

"I came to say that I may have been a little hasty the other day. In spite of that unfortunate incident with the dog I've decided to let you go on weeding my garden."

For a moment Sam was too surprised to speak. But then, just as she opened her mouth to tell Mrs Bratby no thanks, she had another job now, she saw a small, black-and-white face appear at the open window directly behind the sofa.

"The fact is," Mrs Bratby continued, "this morning my garden was attacked by a goat. Really, these people who can't control their animals make my blood boil! But there, the damage is done, and now I want to get it repaired as soon as possible."

"You want me to repair your garden?" asked Sam, transfixed by the sight of Jilly placing her two front legs over the low window-sill.

"I certainly do," said Mrs Bratby. "And I've already told your headmaster that I intend to re-employ you." She smiled smugly. "He said he was most grateful to me for continuing to support his community service scheme. It's not everyone, you know, who's prepared to let children come and work for them."

"Er – no," said Sam, who wasn't even listening. Jilly must have broken free from her tether – and now she had spotted the flowers on Mrs Bratby's hat. Sam watched in horror as the goat stuck out her neck and started nibbling on one of the large pink roses. Next minute...

SNAP!

Jilly had snatched the hat from Mrs Bratby's head.

Chapter 7

Saving Dad's Life

"My hat!" shrieked Mrs Bratby. "Who took my hat?"

She swung round to look behind her, just in time to see Jilly disappear from the window.

"It's that goat again! And it's got MY HAT!"

Sam, who for a horrified minute had

been turned to stone, came back to life. "It's all right, Mrs Bratby. I'll get it for you. Stay here..." She dashed from the room.

"What's happening?" Matthew asked as she ran past the others, who were still trying to listen at the door.

"Jilly's nicked Mrs Bratby's hat ... and I think she's going to eat it!"

Sam raced through the kitchen and out of the back door. Her father looked up in astonishment, especially when she was followed by three other children he had vaguely noticed lurking in the hall.

Seconds later Mrs Bratby swept into the kitchen, her face scarlet with fury. "Where is it?" she demanded. "Where's that wretched goat?"

"Goat? What goat?" Dad asked, bewildered.

"The goat that ate my roses ... and now it's stolen my hat!" She marched past him and out of the back door.

Goats? Hats? A slow smile spread over Dad's face. He grabbed his pad and pencil and followed Mrs Bratby into the garden.

Here he was greeted by the most amazing sight. One small, black-and-white goat, with a flowered hat sticking

out of its mouth, was being pursued by a large, hotly-perspiring lady and four yelling children.

"Jilly, come back..."

"Quick, Sam – grab the rope!"

"I've got it! No, she's got away again..."

"Look out, she's making for the hedge!"

"My hat, my hat!"

This last shout came from Mrs Bratby, who in desperation threw herself at the goat and grabbed one side of her hat. She tried to pull it out of Jilly's mouth, but Jilly wouldn't let go. So the two of them had a tug-of-war, Mrs Bratby holding on to her hat for all she was worth.

"Brilliant!" said Dad, sketching away frantically on his notepad. "Don't stop. Keep pulling, both of you. I want to get this down on paper."

Mrs Bratby tugged even harder. "Give me back – my hat, you – horrible – little –"

"It's okay!" Matthew grabbed the frayed piece of rope still attached to Jilly's collar. "I've got her."

Which was just as well, because a second later there came a loud tearing noise as Jilly finally succeeded in detaching the rose from Mrs Bratby's hat.

"Don't let her eat it," Jovan warned. "It's not a real flower. It could be poisonous."

"It's nothing of the sort," snapped Mrs Bratby. "Do you think I'd go around wearing poisonous flowers on my head? It's the very best quality plastic."

It didn't matter anyway, because Jilly had spat the flower out in disgust. It was the only thing she had refused to eat all day.

Mrs Bratby thrust her de-flowered hat under Dad's nose. "Look at this!" she commanded. "Look at the damage your goat has done. I shall sue—"

"Actually," said Dad, "it's not our goat."

"Actually it is," said Sam, flushing. "Her owner doesn't seem to want her back. Sorry, Dad."

"Ah," said Dad. He put down his notepad and pulled out his wallet. "In that case I'd better pay for the damage. How much was the hat worth? Five pounds?"

"*Five pounds?*" Mrs Bratby looked shocked. "It cost me a great deal more than that, I can tell you."

"Ten? Twenty?"

"It matches my dress. I shall never be able to replace it."

"Twenty-five – and that's my final offer."

Mrs Bratby sniffed. "Oh, very well." She snatched the notes out of his hand. "But I warn you, if I have any more trouble from that goat I shall report you to the police. Now, how do I get out of this wilderness you call a garden?"

"I'll show you." Sam hastily guided her back through the house to the front door. "Er, Mrs Bratby … about the gardening. I'm afraid—"

"Forget it," snapped Mrs Bratby. "And you can be sure Mr Grantham will hear my opinion of his stupid community service scheme. I should have known children could never be relied upon to do anything useful. Pah!"

She stalked off down the path.

Sam closed the door behind her and returned to the garden. Here she found Jilly grazing at the end of a shortened piece of rope while Matthew, Jovan and Katie stood behind Dad, watching him draw.

"Mrs Bratby's going to complain to Mr Grantham," she said despondently. "I reckon we're going to *lose* points instead of getting them. And twenty-five pounds for that stupid hat! I'm sorry, Dad."

"No need to apologize," said her father. "It was worth every penny. In fact I'd go so far as to say that you kids – including Jilly – have saved my life."

Sam looked over his shoulder at the drawing. "You're going to put her in a comic strip, right?"

"Partly right. I'm going to put *all* of you in a comic strip. You'd better tell me more about this Petsitters Club. It sounds an interesting idea."

"We thought it was a good idea too, at the beginning," said Matthew. "But things have gone a bit wrong over Jilly."

Jovan cleared his throat. "My dad told me about a man called Pete Duffy, who keeps a herd of goats on some land at the end of Station Road. He said if we asked him he might find room for one more."

"Jilly would love that!" said Katie. "She'd have lots of company all day long."

"Sounds like the answer," said Dad. "You'd better take her round there and ask him if he's got room for another goat. And if Mrs Jones has a change of heart you can always tell her where Jilly can be found."

Sam couldn't help feeling sad as they walked with Jilly through the streets to Station Road. But Mr Duffy seemed a kindly man and Jilly looked so delighted when she joined the other goats that it was clearly the best solution.

"We've definitely done the right thing," Matthew said, as they walked back home. "I reckon she'll be far better off there than mowing the lawn for Mrs Jones."

"Yes, she will," Sam agreed, cheering up. "It's a real service, our Petsitters Club. After all, animals need helping just as much as humans."

"More," said Katie.

Even Jovan began to feel it might not be too bad, belonging to the Petsitters Club. After all, *he* was the one who had found Jilly a home.

Matthew sighed. "The trouble is we didn't get Mrs Jones to sign the community service form."

"We should have got Jilly to do it," said Katie. "She could have signed it with her hoofprint."

"Don't be daft!" said Matthew. "She'd probably have eaten it."

Sam grinned. "Anyway, points aren't everything. Come on, Petsitters. Let's see if there've been any more messages for us."

The End